The Christmas Tree That Grew

P9-BZC-430

By Phyllis Krasilovsky
Illustrated by Kathy Wilburn

A GOLDEN BOOK • NEW YORK
Western Publishing Company, Inc., Racine, Wisconsin 53404

Copyright © 1987 Phyllis Krasilovsky. Illustrations copyright © 1989 Kathy Wilburn. All rights reserved.
Printed in the U.S.A. No part of this book may be reproduced or copied in any form without written permission
from the publisher. GOLDEN®, GOLDEN & DESIGN®, A GOLDEN BOOK®, and A LITTLE GOLDEN BOOK® are trademarks
of Western Publishing Company, Inc. Library of Congress Catalog Card Number: 88-50810 ISBN: 0-307-00458-9
A B C D E F G H I J K L M

Margaret and Peter Adam were sister and brother. Margaret had straight hair and bangs and Peter had curly hair. Peter often had his nose in a book, while Margaret liked to be active.

They lived with their mother and father in a tiny apartment in a small, narrow house in the city.

There were neighbors in the building, but the people who lived there didn't know each other very well. They lived on separate floors. The Adam family lived on the first floor, which was lucky. They didn't have to climb too many steps.

An old lady named Mrs. Manning lived on the second floor.

Mr. and Mrs. Martinez and their baby daughter lived on the third floor.

Every year Mr. Adam brought home a Christmas tree. The tree took up a lot of room. The Adam family had to move the furniture around so it could fit into their living room. They didn't mind. They loved having a Christmas tree.

They enjoyed decorating it. They hung red candy canes, little toys, and bright-colored balls on it. Mr. Adam strung up red, green, blue, and orange lights. The lights turned on and off like magic. It made the living room look very special.

One year, when the Adam family was planning to move
to a new house in the country after Christmas, Mr. Adam
brought home a live tree. Its roots were tied up in a big ball
of burlap. They had to put it into a big tub and water it to
keep it alive. Mr. Adam said they would plant it in their
new garden.

They decorated the tree just like all the others and hid the burlap-covered roots with red material.

The tree looked beautiful, and it smelled as fresh as a pine forest. They imagined how nice it would be when it was covered with snow, and when the birds came to sit on its branches, in the garden of their new home.

Every morning, before the children went to school,
they took turns watering it. It was nice having a live tree,
because it made Christmas last longer!

One morning, when Margaret went to water the tree, she
noticed that it seemed bigger. When she told her family, they
all went to see. No, they said, she was only imagining it.

When Peter watered the tree, he, too, thought it had grown. Mr. and Mrs. Adam just laughed at the idea, but Margaret agreed with Peter that it had gotten taller.

After that, the children watched the tree very carefully. By the end of the week even Mr. and Mrs. Adam had to agree that it really was taller. The decorations were not as close together as they had been before. Still, the family wanted to keep the tree alive, so they kept watering it.

In a few days the star at the top touched the ceiling! Mr. Adam went to see Mrs. Manning, who lived on the second floor. He told her what had happened. "Would you mind if I made a small hole in your floor, so the tree can keep growing? I could patch it up before we move."

Because Mrs. Manning lived alone and had trouble carrying heavy things up the stairs, she missed being able to have a tree. She said she would be delighted to help.

The tree grew right through the ceiling into Mrs. Manning's apartment, and every day it got bigger. When the branches came up to her waist, Mrs. Manning took down the decorations she had saved for years on her closet shelf. She had put them away when her children moved away and her husband died.

Now she was happy to use them again. She hung up some little wooden angels and carved sleds. It made her happy to remember past Christmases with her family. She invited Margaret and Peter to come upstairs and see how it looked.

"It's beautiful!" they said. "It's just like a separate tree!"

Mrs. Manning baked them Christmas cookies, just as she had done for her own children. She gave them apple cider to drink and told them stories about her other Christmases. It was just like a party. Almost every afternoon they went upstairs to visit her, to see the tree, and to eat more cookies.

One day, when they went upstairs, they were astonished
to see that the tree was touching Mrs. Manning's ceiling! She
was worried, because there was no more room for it to grow.

Mr. Adam asked Mr. and Mrs. Martinez if he might drill a hole in their third-floor living room.

Mr. Martinez had lost his job as a carpenter, so he didn't have money to buy a tree. Mr. Martinez was happy to help Mr. Adam drill a nice even circle in the floor.

Mr. Adam was very impressed with how neatly Mr. Martinez worked. He asked him if he would like to build bookcases for the Adam family's new house. Mr. Martinez was glad to have some work. He went with Mr. Adam to the new house to take measurements.

Mr. and Mrs. Martinez eagerly watched the tree grow into their apartment. Mrs. Martinez made popcorn necklaces and strung them on the branches as they came through the floor. When the tree got higher, she added balls of bright-colored knitting yarn and painted nuts hung on bits of red ribbon.

When Margaret and Peter went upstairs to see it, they were thrilled. Mrs. Martinez offered them leftover popcorn and nuts. They ate happily and played with her baby. The baby gurgled and laughed at all the attention.

Almost every day now the children went up and down to visit Mrs. Manning and the Martinez family, for they had all become good friends because of the tree.

The day before Christmas it snowed so hard that no one could go outside.

Mr. and Mrs. Adam invited Mrs. Manning and the Martinez family for Christmas dinner. What a nice time they had! They were just like one big family. The bright lights on the tree made the Martinez baby laugh.

After dinner they sang Christmas songs. Then they all went upstairs, first to Mrs. Manning's and then to the Martinez apartment, to admire the tree once again.

A few days later the Adam family moved to their country house. They took the tree down and brought it with them. Mr. Martinez patched up the two ceilings and helped to load the new bookcases he had built. He was happy because Mr. Adam had helped him find a new job in a furniture store.

Mr. Adam planted the tree in a hole he had dug in the garden. It looked very beautiful. Two cardinals came to sit on a branch almost immediately!

One Sunday Mrs. Manning and the Martinez family came to visit the Adams in their new house. They brought presents. Mrs. Manning had made balls of suet rolled in pumpkin seeds to hang on the tree branches for the birds. Mr. Martinez had built a fine bird-feeding station and a birdhouse. "These are to thank you for sharing your Christmas tree with us," they said.

Mr. and Mrs. Adam said, "Thank YOU! You must come for Christmas dinner next year, to share the tree again. After all, it gave us new friends."

Margaret and Peter just beamed with happiness.